For Tom Tom and Oka, who both have a gift
for spreading happiness — C.C.

To my cat, Benito, and my dogs, Elvis and Kika.
Thanks for all the moments of happy company — C.V.

This book belongs to

_____

The illustrations in this book were created using coloured pencils and digital methods.

First published in 2023 by Floris Books. Text © 2023 Caroline Crowe. Illustrations © 2023 Carlos Vélez. Caroline Crowe and Carlos Vélez have asserted their right under the Copyright, Designs and Patent Act 1988 to be identified as the Author and Illustrator of this Work All rights reserved. No part of this book may be reproduced without the prior permission of Floris Books, Edinburgh www.florisbooks.co.uk British Library CIP data available
ISBN 978-178250-832-8 Printed in China through Imago

Printed on sustainably sourced FSC® certified paper. Uses plant-based inks which reduces chemical emissions.

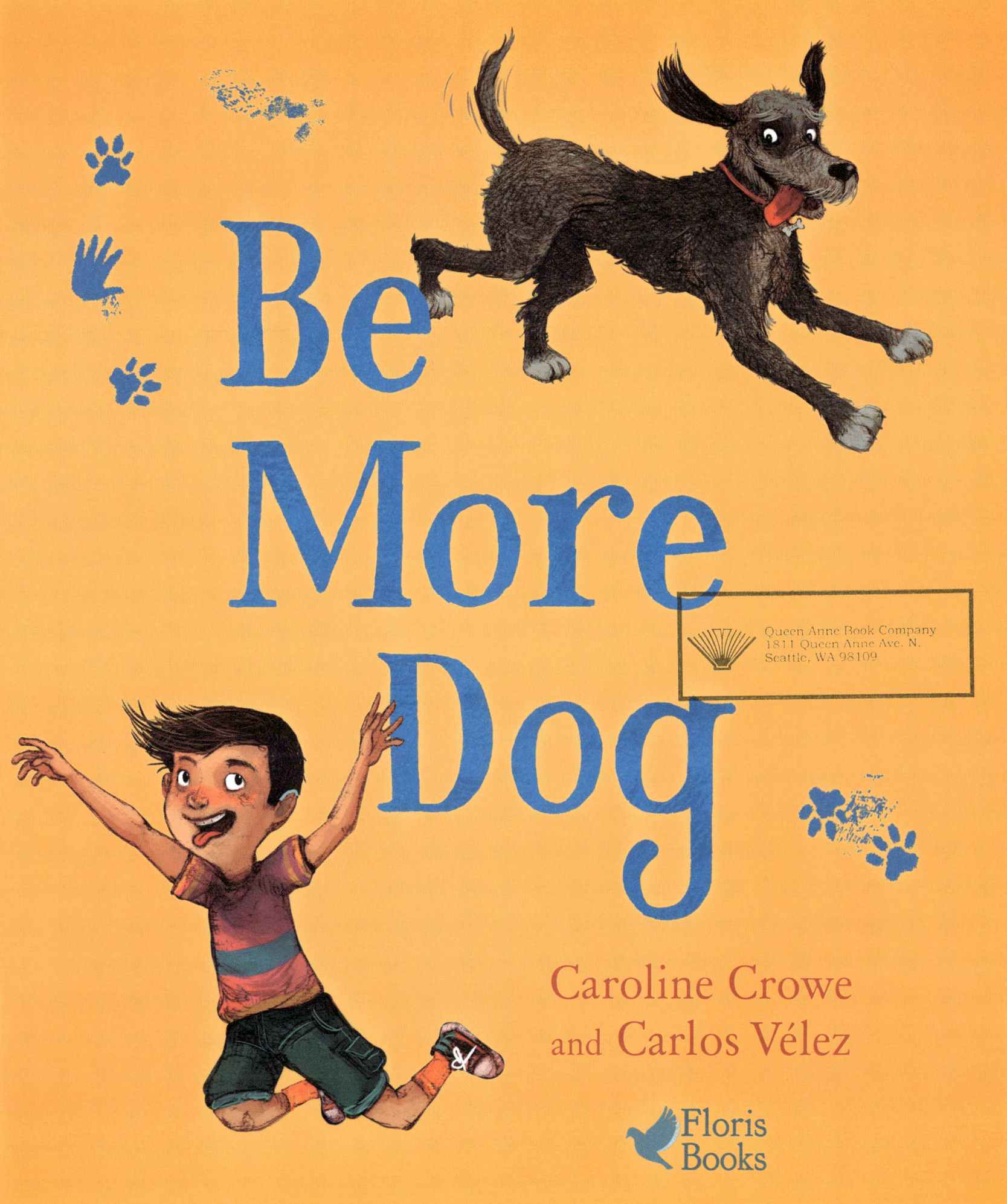

My dog Sam has a superpower.

He doesn't wear a costume.

He can't fly.

And he definitely can't make himself invisible.

Sam's superpower is happiness.
His tail **NEVER** stops wagging.

This morning Dad went to work, and I'm worried my happiness got packed in his bag. Because when he left, I think my happiness went with him.

So I'm going to follow Sam, because if anyone can help me find it, he can.

First, we sniff the morning. It smells of grass and fresh air.

Then we sniff Dad's old boot. That makes Sam happy…

But I prefer Granny's baking!

At the park, Sam shows me how to chase happiness.

How to lie in wait for it.

And how to **JUMP** up and **CATCH** it!

Then Sam gives me some treasure he finds,
even though I know he'd love to keep it.

I think making me happy makes him happy.

So I give Granny some of my treasure,
and her smile makes me smile.

On our way home happiness appears in a

WHOOSH,

like the rush of wind in our faces.

But then it rains and my smile gets washed away.

Until Sam shows me you can be happy even when it's raining.

After dinner it starts to get dark outside, and Dad still isn't home.

But Sam isn't worried. He's doing something that always makes him happy instead.

So I do something that always makes me happy too.

Then we hear the front door opening...

…and happiness sweeps us up like a **GIGANTIC WAVE**.

Thanks to Sam, I know I can find happiness on my own now.

But it's even better finding it together.

Sam has shown me that happiness is all around us.

Sometimes you just have to be more dog to find it.

Caroline Crowe is an award-winning children's author from the UK. She was a newspaper journalist for many years and can't believe she now gets to write children's stories as her job. Her picture books include *Our Incredible Library Book*, *The Fairy Dogmother* and *Tiny Tantrum*. She lives with her young family in Hampshire, England.

Carlos Vélez is an award-winning illustrator from Mexico. He is the illustrator of more than twenty children's books, including *A Billion Balloons of Questions*, *Three Lines in a Circle* and *We Belong*. Carlos currently lives in Coyoacán, Mexico.